Chapter 1

"Here we are, gang," Fred said. "The Palace Theatre." He steered the Mystery Machine into a parking space across the street from the theatre.

"Like, it's about time," Shaggy said.

"What's the matter, Shaggy?" Daphne asked. "Don't want to be late for the piano concert?"

"No, I don't want to be late for the food," Shaggy replied. "Like, I'm starving."

"Me roo," Scooby-Doo agreed, nodding.

Fred looked at the tickets in his hand. "These tickets we won from the radio station say that the concert starts after the reception."

"So, like, when does the reception start?" Shaggy asked.

Fred looked at the tickets and then at his watch. "Right now."

"Then what are we standing around for?" Shaggy said. "Let's move our feet across the street 'cause Scooby and I have food to eat!"

The gang got out of the van and walked across the street. Outside of the theatre a few teenagers were holding signs that read SAVE THE PALACE.

"What's going on?" Velma asked.

But before anyone could answer, a limousine pulled up. A tall man dressed in a tuxedo got out of the car, and the crowd started booing. The man waved to the crowd and quickly walked into the theatre.

"Golly, I wonder what he did to make those people so mad," Daphne said. "Whatever it was, it must be pretty bad," Velma added.

"Excuse me," Fred said to one of the teenagers. "Why

did all of you boo that man?"

"Like, that guy is a total sellout," the teenager replied. "He betrayed us and, like, his music to make money."

"Like, huh?" Shaggy said.

A teenage girl next to the boy turned around.

"Todd, I'll explain," she said to him and then looked at Shaggy and his friends. "My name's Lisa, and we're here to save the Palace Theatre. We don't want to see the place torn down."

"That's right, man," Todd said. "And that sellout guy in the limo was Stuart Banyon."

"Who's Stuart Banyon?" Daphne asked.

"You probably know him by the name Sloop," Lisa added.

"Like, you mean Sloop Banyon, the rock star?" Shaggy asked. "That was him? Wow! This is going to be some concert after all!"

"Wait a second," Velma said. "I thought Sloop Banyon stopped performing a fewyears ago."

"That's right," Lisa continued. "Once he became a big star and made some money, he started investing in property. He made so much money doing that, he decided to quit rock and roll."

"So what is he doing here now?" Fred asked.

"He's buying up old theatres and turning them into multiplex cinemas," Lisa continued. "They say he wants to tear down the Palace next."

"Jinkies," Velma said. "That sounds like a really rotten thing to do."

"Especially since he got his big break as a rock

star at this theatre," Lisa added. "That's why my friends and I are protesting."

"Excuse me," Shaggy interrupted, "but if Sloop Banyon doesn't perform anymore, then, like, who's doing the concert?"

"Some totally buttoned-down, nerded-out concert pianist," Todd said.

"Ruh?" Scooby said.

"Hugo Frescanini, the world-famous concert pianist," Velma said.

"Sounds boring to me," Shaggy said. "But then Scooby and I can eat to any kind of music. Right, Scoob?"

"Right!" Scooby barked, wagging his tail.

"Then let's go," Shaggy said. "To the food!"

"Roo the rood!" Scooby echoed.

Chapter 2

The gang walked into the Palace Theatre. "Jinkies," Velma said. "Look at the size of this lobby."

Large posters of famous old films and performers lined the walls of the large room. Directly over the centre of the lobby hung an enormous crystal chandelier. The lobby was full of people walking around and chatting, waiting for the concert to begin.

"If this is the size of the lobby," Fred said, "I can't imagine the size of the theatre itself."

"And Scooby and I can't imagine the size of the feast," Shaggy added. "Speaking of food, like, which way to the buffet?"

"Reah, rich ray?" Scooby repeated.

"It's right over there, under the film poster for *The Sands of Cairo*," a man said behind them. The gang turned around.

"I'm Melvin Snorkelmuch," he said. "I'm the owner."

"We're pleased to meet you, sir," Daphne said. "We were just admiring the theatre lobby. Everything is so beautiful."

"Thank you," Melvin replied. "I take great pride in how well the Palace is maintained. It's the oldest and biggest theatre in the area, you know. Of course, if I don't find some big talent, it will all be for nothing. I'm going to have to close down and sell the place."

"To Sloop Banyon?" Velma asked.

Melvin nodded sadly. "Yes, Sloop Banyon," he sighed. "I gave him his big break all those years ago. And how does he thank me? By trying to buy the theatre so he can turn it into a multiplex."

"If he wants to tear down the theatre," Daphne said, "why would he come to a concert that's trying to save it?"

"Because I'm a big fan of Hugo Frescanini," someone said behind them.

Everyone turned around and saw the tall man who had been in the limousine.

"Like, it's really Sloop Banyon, in the flesh," Shaggy said.

"*Stuart* Banyon," the man said, correcting him. "I haven't used the name Sloop in quite some time. It doesn't really work in the property world. And like I said, I'm here because I'm a fan of Hugo Frescanini. He's the best performer you've ever had here, Melvin. Since me, that is."

Stuart Banyon waved to someone across the room and quickly walked away.

"Gee, he sure wasn't very nice," Daphne said.

"Forget about him," Melvin said. "Let's concentrate on tonight."

"Speaking of tonight, Mr. Snuckle-morch," Shaggy began, "like, where did you say the food is?"

"Right over there," Melvin said, pointing towards the film poster. "There's lots of food so feel free to dig in. And by the way, my name is *Snorkelmuch*."

"Sorry about that, man," Shaggy said. "And we'll see you guys later," he said to the others. Shaggy and Scooby started to walk towards the food.

"Stay out of trouble, you two," Daphne said.

"Like, we're just going to grab a snack," Shaggy said. "What kind of trouble could we possibly get into?"

"I don't know," Fred replied. "But we don't want to find out."

Chapter 3

Shaggy and Scooby-Doo walked across the lobby to the buffet. They each picked up a plate.

"You know what Mr. Snuchenorkle said, Scooby," Shaggy said.

"Rig in!" Scooby barked happily. They started moving down the buffet line, piling their plates high with a little bit of everything on the table. When they reached the end, their plates were so full they couldn't see over the top.

"Like, Scooby-Doo," Shaggy called. "Where are you?"

"Rover rere," Scooby answered. He was standing right next to Shaggy, but neither one of them could see over the piles of food on their plates.

"I guess there's only one thing we can do now," Shaggy said.

"Eat!" they sang together.

In less than a minute, Shaggy and Scooby had licked their plates clean.

"There you are, Scooby-Doo," Shaggy said now that his view was not blocked by food. "Ready for seconds?"

"Rou ret!" Scooby barked. This time, there was a short queue at the buffet table. Shaggy and

Scooby stood next to a woman dressed in a blue suit with white lines, numbers, and shapes all over it.

"Hey, Scooby," Shaggy whispered, "get a load of Madame Blueprint over here. I think she's wearing the plans for a town house."

"Ror a roghouse," Scooby joked. Shaggy and Scooby giggled until the woman turned around.

"Actually, they're the blueprints for this theatre," she said. "I had a designer friend of mine copy the blueprints onto fabric."

Just then, Daphne, Fred, and Velma walked up to the buffet queue.

"I think your outfit is groovy," Daphne said. "I noticed it from across the room."

"Thank you," the woman said. "My name's Wanda Weathers. I'm an architect in town. This outfit is my tribute to this wonderful old theatre."

"So you agree with those people carrying the signs outside?" Fred asked.

"Heavens no," Wanda replied. "This is a wonderful old theatre, but one that has outlived its usefulness."

"What do you mean?" Daphne asked. "This lobby is beautiful."

"Beautiful but drafty," Wanda answered. "And the theatre itself? Half the seats are broken. The heating needs to be replaced. The floor is sagging. They even had to close off the balcony because the plaster is falling off the ceiling. The best thing for this theatre is for it to be torn down."

"How do you know so much about this theatre?" Velma asked.

"I'm an architect, and I did a study of this theatre just a few days ago," Wanda said. "Now, if you'll excuse me, I need to go find a client of mine. He's around here somewhere."

Wanda walked away as Shaggy and Scooby reached the front of the queue. They each picked up another plate. Just as they were about to start piling on the food, a loud noise shook the room.

"Rikes!" Scooby barked as he dove under the buffet table.

"Come on, Scoob," Shaggy said. "Are you going to let a little noise stand in the way of this beautiful buffet?"

Another loud noise echoed through the room. Everyone covered their ears.

"Zoinks!" Shaggy cried. "Make room for me, Scoob." He dove under the table, too.

"What is that noise?" Daphne asked.

"It sounds like an electric guitar," Fred said.

"Amplified very loudly," Velma added.

"Where is it coming from?" Daphne asked.

"I don't know, but it looks like Mr. Snorkelmuch is going to try to find out," Velma noticed.

"Then I say we should, too," Fred said. "Let's go." The three of them followed Melvin to one end of the lobby and walked through an unmarked door.

"Wait for us!" Shaggy called from under the table. He and Scooby popped up and looked around. "Like, which way did they go? How are we going to find them?"

Scooby thought for a moment.

"Rollow me!" he barked. Scooby put his nose to the ground and started sniffing around. He found a scent and followed it to the big staircase in the middle of the lobby. Shaggy was close behind.

"Leave it to Scooby-Doo," he said. "The nose always knows."

Chapter 4

Fred, Daphne, and Velma followed Melvin down a long corridor. At the end, they walked through a door and found themselves backstage. The curtain was down so they couldn't see the seats in the audience. Onstage, they saw Mevin speaking to an older man, who was wearing brown trousers, a tan shirt, and an old brown waistcoat. They were standing next to a grand piano.

"Gus, you've got to do something," Melvin pleaded. "You know this place inside and out. Can't you find where that music was coming from?"

"I've worked here thirty-five years," Gus said, "and I've seen a lot of things. But I've never seen anything like this. Sounds to me like we've got ourselves a ghost."

"There's no such thing as ghosts," Velma said.

Melvin and Gus turned and saw her standing with Fred and Daphne.

"Maybe, and maybe not, young lady," Gus said. "All I know is that strange things have been happening around here the past few days."

"Really?" Daphne asked. "Like what?"

"Oh, a sandbag came loose from the rafters and made a hole in the stage," Gus explained. "And then the curtain got stuck halfway up. Wouldn't budge."

"Those things happened because this theatre

is so old," Melvin said. "There's no ghost here. The concert is supposed to begin soon. Gus, please take a look around and see what you can find. Just be back in time to raise the curtain."

"All right, I'll look around," Gus said. "But I'm not making any promises. I'm a stage manager, not a ghost detective." Gus turned and walked offstage, muttering to himself.

"I have to check on Mr. Frescanini," Melvin said. "Why don't you kids find your seats? The audience should be coming in soon." Melvin turned and walked backstage to the dressing rooms.

"Hey," Fred said, "where are Shaggy and Scooby?"

"I thought they were right behind us," Daphne said.

"Hello down there!" Shaggy called. His voice echoed throughout the theatre.

Everyone onstage looked around to try to find where Shaggy's voice was coming from.

"Shaggy?" Velma called. "Scooby-Doo? Where are you?"

Fred, Daphne, and Velma stepped in front of the curtain.

"Rover rere!" Scooby barked, his voice also echoing throughout the theatre.

"Like, we're in the balcony!" Shaggy called down.

"What are you doing up in the balcony?" Daphne called back.

"We were looking for you," Shaggy replied. "We took a wrong turn and ended up here.

We'll be right down!"

"We'll meet you at the seats," Fred called back.

Shaggy turned to Scooby. "Let's go, pal," he
said. He and Scooby walked towards the exit. They
walked through the doorway and started down the
big staircase. When they were halfway down, they
heard some music coming from behind them.

"Uh, Scooby, did you bring a radio with you?"
Shaggy asked.

"Ruh-uh," Scooby said, shaking his head.

They slowly turned around and saw a ghost
standing at the top of the stairs. It was tall and
wearing sunglasses and playing an electric guitar.

"Zoinks! A ghost! A ghost!" Shaggy cried.

"Rikes!" Scooby barked.

"Come on, Scoob, let's get out of here!" Shaggy and Scooby ran down the stairs as fast as they could. When they got to the lobby, they saw that everyone had already gone into the theatre for the concert.

"Like, everyone's inside," Shaggy said. "We have to tell the others. I just hope we're not too late."

Chapter 5

Inside the theatre auditorium, the piano recital was about to begin. Shaggy and Scooby quietly opened the doors and stepped inside. They looked around, trying to find Fred, Daphne, and Velma.

"Like, the backs of everyone's heads look the same," Shaggy said. "We'll never find them."

"Rollow me!" Scooby said. He put his nose to the ground and started sniffing.

"Oh, no, not again," Shaggy said. "The last time we followed your nose we ended up seeing a ghost. This time we're going to use my eyes. It's bright enough in here that I should be able to spot them in no time."

The lights in the theatre dimmed.

"Unless, like, they turn off the lights," Shaggy said.

Melvin Snorkelmuch walked out onstage. The people in the audience started clapping.

"Thank you, ladies and gentlemen," Melvin said. "It is my pleasure to welcome you to the Palace Theatre. I want to thank you for your generous support in helping us keep this wonderful old theatre open. And now, without further ado, the Palace Theatre is proud to present the world-famous concert pianist, Hugo Frescanini!"

Melvin walked off the stage as the curtain rose. The audience applauded loudly. Onstage, a short man wearing a tuxedo stood next to the grand piano. Hugo Frescanini bowed and sat down behind the keyboard. He raised his fingers over the piano keys. The audience was completely silent. Even Shaggy and Scooby were quiet. Hugo Frescanini brought his fingers down on the keys.

Suddenly a big burst of smoke filled the stage. Everyone gasped. When the smoke cleared, the ghost was standing on the stage, next to the piano.

"Zoinks! It's that ghost again!" Shaggy exclaimed.

The ghost raised his hand and played a chord on his electric guitar. The music echoed throughout the theatre. It was the same sound everyone had heard out in the lobby. This time, the ghost started playing a song. The music was very loud. As he played, the ghost sang in a strange, echoing voice:

You all must leave!
This place must close!
Listen to what I say:
I'll haunt the Palace
With music and malice
Forever and ever and a day.

"Like, if he weren't a ghost," Shaggy said, "he wouldn't be a bad rock star!"

As the ghost played the final chord of the song on his guitar, another puff of smoke filled the stage. When the smoke cleared, the ghost was gone, and so was Hugo Frescanini.

Everyone in the audience jumped up and started running out of the theatre.

"Now how are we going to find the others?" Shaggy said.

"Rup rere," Scooby said. He jumped up onto Shaggy's shoulders so he could see over everything.

"Good thinking, Scoob," Shaggy said.

Melvin ran out onstage. "Ladies and gentlemen," he called, "please remain calm. Everything will be all right." He turned and yelled offstage, "Gus, close the curtain!"
Nothing happened, so Melvin ran offstage to lower the curtain himself.

Fred, Daphne, and Velma stood up from their seats to go backstage, too. Scooby saw them get up.

"Ret's ro, Raggy!" he barked. "Ris ray!" He guided Shaggy through the crowd and caught up with Fred, Daphne, and Velma. When they all got backstage, Melvin was sitting on a stool next to the curtain ropes.

"Mr Snorkelmuch, are you okay?" Daphne asked.

Before he could answer, they all heard someone moaning.

"Yikes, it's that ghost again!" Shaggy cried. "He keeps following us!"

"That doesn't sound like our guitar-playing ghost," Velma said. "That sounds like a man."

Everyone looked around.

"Over here," Fred called. He was standing beside a piece of scenery. He reached behind it and helped guide Gus out. Gus was holding his head.

"Gus, are you all right?" Melvin asked as he ran over to him. He helped Gus walk over to the stool.

"Of course I'm not all right," Gus said angrily. "Something hit me on the head. I told you a million times this place is falling apart and that you should just sell it. Heaven knows I could use the rest."

"I don't know what to do anymore,"
Melvin said. "I may as well close up right
now. Once word gets out about this ghost and
what happened to Hugo Frescanini, I'll be forced to
shut down for sure."

Fred motioned for the rest of the gang to
huddle around him. They whispered among
themselves for a moment.

"Mr Snorkelmuch," Fred said, "give us a
chance to get to the bottom of this."

"I don't know ... ." Melvin said.

"Look at it this way," Daphne said.
"You've got nothing to lose."

Melvin thought for a moment. "Why not? I'll do anything to keep all of this under wraps."

"Don't worry, Mr Snorkelmuch," Velma said. "You won't be sorry."

"Let's get you to my office where you can lie down, Gus," Melvin said, leading Gus away.

When they were gone, Fred turned to the others. "Gang, it's time to get to work," he said.

Chapter 6

I want to check out the balcony stairs where Shaggy and Scooby say they saw the ghost," Fred said.

"Great idea, Fred," Daphne said. "I'll go with you."

"Shaggy, Scooby, and I will look around the stage," Velma said. "We're bound to find some clues here."

"Okay, we'll meet back here as soon as we're done," Daphne replied. Fred and Daphne walked out from backstage and headed for the balcony stairs. Velma looked around the stage area for a moment.

"You two see if you can find any clues onstage," she said. "I'm going to see if I can find anything back where we found Gus." Velma walked offstage and started looking around behind the backdrop.

Shaggy and Scooby looked around the stage for a minute.

"Psst, hey, Scooby," Shaggy whispered. "I have an idea. Go and sit at the piano and wait for my cue."

"Rokay," Scooby said. He walked over and sat on the piano bench.

"Ladies and gentlemen," Shaggy said, "it is my great pleasure to present the world-famous concert pianist, Scooby-Dooberini." Shaggy pulled the ropes that raised the curtain. Then he pulled down the locking lever to keep the curtain from closing. "Boy, this curtain is heavier than it looks," he said.

Scooby looked out at the empty theatre and bowed. Then he raised his paws over the piano and started banging out notes. Shaggy covered his ears and walked over to the piano.

"Here, Scooby-Dooberini, let me show you some real music," Shaggy said, sitting down next

to Scooby. Shaggy started playing "Chopsticks."
Soon, Scooby joined in and they played together.
They were having so much fun they didn't see
Velma walk onto the stage.
She was about to scold
Shaggy and Scooby when
she noticed something on
the floor.

   "Hey, what's this?" she
said, bending down. Velma
picked up a piece of paper.
   Scooby and Shaggy
didn't hear her because they
were still playing the piano.

"Would you two knock it off?" Velma asked. "You're supposed to be looking for clues."

"Just one more note, Velma," Shaggy said. "Ready for the big finish, Scoob?" The two of them raised their hands and paws and hit the piano keys for a final chord. Just as they did, a puff of smoke filled the stage and they heard Velma scream. When the smoke cleared, Velma was gone.

"Zoinks! Like, our music must have blown her away," Shaggy said. "Velma? Velma, like, where'd you go?" Shaggy called.

"Relma?" Scooby barked.

Shaggy and Scooby jumped off the piano bench and looked around.

"Oh, no," Shaggy said, "we'd better get the others. I think the ghost got Velma!"

"Relp! Relp!" Scooby barked.

A moment later, Fred and Daphne ran onstage. "What is it?" Fred asked.

"It's Velma!" Shaggy said.

"What about her?" Daphne asked.

"She's gone!" Shaggy answered.

"What? How?" Fred said.

"Like, Scooby and I were playing the piano and Velma was standing right there. All of a

sudden, there was a big puff of smoke and the next thing we knew, Velma was gone."

"I hope she's all right," Daphne said.

"I'm fine!" Velma called. She sounded far away.

"Velma? Where are you?" Fred called back.

"I'm up here, in the balcony," Velma replied. "Wait right there. I have some clues to show you!"

Chapter 7

A few moments later, Velma joined the others onstage.

"Like, Velma, are you okay?" Shaggy asked.

"I'm fine, Shaggy," Velma said.

"What happened?" Fred asked. "And how did you get all the way up to the balcony?"

"I was standing on the stage by the piano," Velma explained. "And the next thing I knew, I felt the floor give way. I landed on a pile of pillows. It was a little dark, so I kept my hand along the wall. I followed some steps and I ended up in the balcony."

"Jeepers, a secret passage," Daphne said. "That explains a lot."

"So does what we found," Fred said. "At the top of the stairs, Daphne and I noticed some wires coming out from under the carpeting. They were stereo speaker wires, and they led into the wall behind one of the posters."

"Like, how about that?" Shaggy said. "Our ghost is wired for sound." He and Scooby giggled.

"Well, that's not all," Velma continued. "Just before I took my little journey, I found this on the stage." Velma held up a ticket to the concert.

"I have a hunch that our guitar-playing ghost is about to be unplugged," Fred said.

"You're right, Fred," Velma replied.

"It's time to set a trap," Fred said. "So here's the plan. Shaggy and I will hide behind the backdrop. Scooby, you'll sit at the piano, pretending to be another concert pianist. When the ghost appears, Shaggy and I will throw the piano cover over him."

"Like, how do you know the ghost will come back?" Shaggy asked. "Maybe he doesn't do two shows a night."

"If he really wants us out of this theatre, he'll come back," Fred explained. "Especially if he thinks that Scooby is going to give the concert that Hugo Frescanini was supposed to."

"Like, all this sounds good except for one thing," Shaggy said.

"What's that?" Fred asked.

"Your plan hit a sour note with our concert pianist over there," Shaggy replied. He pointed to Scooby-Doo, who was sitting with his paws crossed.

"Come on, Scooby," Daphne said. "Won't you help us out?"

Scooby turned his head away. "Ruh-uh," he said.

"Will you do it for a Scooby Snack?" Velma asked.

Scooby didn't move.

"How about two Scooby Snacks?" Fred said.

Scooby shook his head.

40

"How about three Scooby Snacks?" Daphne said, holding out three treats.

"Like, *I'll* do it for three Scooby Snacks," Shaggy said.

"Roh way!" Scooby barked. He jumped in front of Shaggy and gobbled the snacks out of Daphne's hand. "Scooby-Dooby-Doo!" he barked.

"Good boy, Scooby," Daphne said.

"I'll go get Mr Snorkelmuch," Fred said. "This

way it will look more realistic. In the meantime, Shaggy, you help Scooby get dressed for the part."

"And while you do that," Velma added, "Daphne and I will take another visit to that secret passage. I have a feeling there's more back there than meets the eye."

"Sounds like a plan to me," Fred said. "Let's go!"

Chapter 8

Fred walked back onstage with Melvin Snorkelmuch.

"Are you sure your plan will work?" Melvin asked.

"Absolutely," Fred said. "By the way, I didn't see Gus in your office. Is he all right?"

"Oh, yes," Melvin explained. "He wanted to go home, so he left a short while ago."

"I see," Fred said. "Shaggy! Scooby! Where are you?"

"Like, you can't rush a concert pianist,"
Shaggy said. "The great Dooberini will be right
out."

Fred asked, "Are you all set, Mr Snorkelmuch?"

"Ready when you are," he replied.

"Then let's take our places," Fred said. "Let's go,
Shaggy."
Fred and Shaggy walked off-stage and hid behind
the scenery. They held the large canvas piano cover
in their hands.

"Oh, Mr Dooberini!" Melvin called. "Are you
ready?"

Scooby-Doo walked out onstage. He was
wearing a grey tuxedo
jacket and a grey
bow tie, and the
fur on top of
his head was
brushed back.

"Thank you
for agreeing
to step in on
such short
notice, Mr
Dooberini,"

44

Melvin said. "It was tragic what happened to Mr Frescanini. We are grateful you will be able to perform the concert in his place."

"Ro roblem," Scooby said.

"Please have a seat and make sure the piano is up to your professional standards," Melvin said to Scooby.

"Rokay!" he barked.

Scooby sat down at the piano. He raised his paws up high and then brought them down gently. He played a fast version of "Chopsticks" and then banged around on the keyboard with his paws. Right after he hit a particularly loud chord, a puff of smoke appeared. When it cleared, the ghost was standing on the stage.

The ghost walked up behind Scooby and played a chord on his electric guitar. The music echoed through the theatre.

"Rikes!" Scooby barked as he jumped up.

"Now!" Fred called. He and Shaggy ran out from behind the backdrop. They threw the piano cover up in the air but the ghost ducked out of the way. The cover came down on Melvin Snorkelmuch. Thinking he was the ghost, Fred and Shaggy accidentally tackled him to the ground.

The ghost started after Scooby, so Scooby ran around the piano. The ghost reached out and grabbed Scooby's jacket. Unable to run, Scooby took his arms out of the jacket, sending the ghost reeling back into the piano. The piano lid slammed shut, trapping the ghost. The noise of the lid scared Scooby so much he ran offstage. He ran right into the curtain rope and knocked the locking lever loose. Scooby's tail got tangled in the curtain rope. He shot straight up as the curtain came crashing down on the trapped ghost.

Chapter 9

Fred and Shaggy helped Melvin out of the piano cover.

"Sorry about that, Mr. Snorkelmuch," Fred said. "I hope you're all right."

"Never mind about me," Melvin said. "Did you get that ghost?"

They looked over at the piano. The ghost was banging on the lid.

"Hey, where's Scooby-Doo?" Shaggy said, looking around.

"Relp, Raggy!" Scooby called. "Rup rere!"

Shaggy, Fred, and Melvin looked up and saw Scooby hanging on to the curtain rope up by the ceiling.

"Scooby-Doo, this is no time for hanging around," Shaggy said. "We caught a ghost."

"I'll help him down," Melvin said. He walked over and raised the curtain slowly. As the curtain went up, Scooby came down.

"Ranks!" said Scooby, giving Melvin a big lick across the face.

Fred walked over to the piano. "Now everyone will see who this groovy ghost really is," Fred said. "Mr. Snorkelmuch, would you like to do the honours?"

"Wait for us!" Velma called. She and Daphne walked onstage with Hugo Frescanini.

"Mr. Frescanini!" Melvin shouted. "Are you all right?"

"I'm fine," the pianist answered. "Thanks to these nice young ladies. Somehow they knew

49

exactly where to find me."

"He was in a small room under the stage," Velma said. "Right off that passageway I found."

"Now let's see who's behind all this," Melvin said. He opened the lid of the piano and pulled off the ghost's sheet.

"Wanda Weathers!" Melvin exclaimed. "I don't believe it!"

"Just as we suspected," Velma said.

"How did you know?" Melvin asked.

"First I found this ticket on the stage right after the ghost and Mr. Frescanini disappeared," Velma explained. "I knew it couldn't be a real ghost because a real ghost wouldn't need a ticket to get in."

"A real ghost also wouldn't need speaker wires to amplify its music," Daphne continued. "The wires we found up in the balcony led to speakers hidden in the walls."

"At first, we thought Sloop Banyon was the ghost," Fred said.

"We thought it was kind of strange that he would come to the same theatre he wanted to tear down," Daphne said.

"But we realized that the ghost knew its way around this theatre pretty well," Fred continued.

"Especially around all the secret passages under the stage," Velma continued. "And how to wire the trapdoor on the stage to the piano keys."

"So that left only two other suspects: Wanda Weathers and Gus," Daphne said.

"It's true that Gus was never around when the ghost appeared," Fred said. "But that bump on his head was real."

"We didn't think he would do that to himself just to avoid suspicion," Daphne added.

"So that left Wanda," Velma said.

"But why?" Melvin asked, turning to the architect.

"Because I needed a big break for my architecture business," Wanda said. "I wanted to scare people away from here so you'd sell to Sloop – I mean Stuart – Banyon. Then I hoped to sell him my plans for the new multiplex."

"I don't think that will be necessary," Stuart Banyon said. He walked down the aisle of the theatre with Todd, Lisa, and a policeman.

"What are you saying?" Melvin asked.

"There's a huge mob of people outside this place," Stuart Banyon said. "And it sounds like they want to buy tickets. Right, kids?"

"Like, it's a total scene, dude," Todd said.

"We all heard about the guitar-playing rock-and-roll ghost," Lisa said. "And we all want to see him."

"You mean there's actually a line of people outside the theatre waiting to come in?" Melvin asked.

"That's right," Lisa said. "Word is spreading about the groovy ghost. I'll bet even more people will come."

"Man, that's too bad, because the ghost is —mmmfmfm," Shaggy said until Melvin put his hand over Shaggy's mouth.

"That's too bad because the ghost isn't going to be able to perform for everybody at once," Melvin said. "But we'll work it out. Maybe we'll do two shows a night. This is wonderful!"

"Well, Mr. Snorkelmuch, it looks like you've found a way to save the Palace Theatre," Fred said.

"No thanks to you nosy kids and your meddling mutt," Wanda muttered.

"Officer, would you mind taking Ms. Weathers to the police station?" Melvin asked. "I'll be down shortly."

The policeman came up onstage and took Wanda Weathers away.

"Good news for you, bad news for me," Stuart Banyon said. "This place would have made a nice multiplex. Good luck, Melvin."

Stuart Banyon turned and left the theatre.

"Thank you, kids, for all of your help," Melvin said. "None of this would have happened without you and your wonderful dog."

"Speaking of our wonderful dog," Velma said. "Where's Scooby-Doo?"

"Looks like he learned a thing or two from the ghost," Shaggy said.

Everyone looked over and saw Scooby wearing the ghost's sunglasses. Todd and Lisa were dancing as Scooby played the guitar.

"Scooby-Groovy-Doo!" he barked.

Everyone laughed as the music played on.

SCOOBY-DOO MYSTERIES

Solve a Mystery With Scooby-Doo!

978-1-782-02155-1

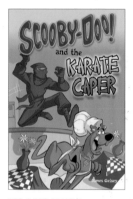

978-1-782-02150-6

978-1-782-02152-0

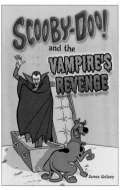

978-1-782-02153-7